MASCOT HEROES

DIANN WALL-WILSON

Copyright 2024 by Angelo Thomas Crapanzano

All rights reserved. This book or any portion thereof may not be reproduced or used in any manner whatsoever without the express written permission of the publisher except for the use of brief quotation in a book review.

ISBN 978-1-964462-78-3 (Paperback)
ISBN 978-1-964462-79-0 (Ebook)

Inquiries and Book Orders should be addressed to:

Leavitt Peak Press
17901 Pioneer Blvd Ste L #298, Artesia, California 90701
Phone #: 2092191548

DEDICATION

THIS BOOK IS DEDICATED TO ALL THOSE BRAVE MEN AND WOMEN WHO SERVE AND HAVE SERVED IN THE UNITED STATES ARMED FORCES. IT IS ALSO DEDICATED TO ALL THOSE BRAVE SOULS WHO SERVED THE UNITED STATES ARMED FORCES WHO GAVE THEIR LIVES FIGHTING GALLANTLY FOR THEIR NATION.

THIS BOOK IS ESPECIALLY DEDICATED TO WILLIAM R. WALL, SR., DIANN WALL WILSON'S FATHER, WHO SERVED IN THE ARMY AND SURVIVED FIVE WWII CAMPAIGNS. IT IS ALSO DEDICATED TO ERIN (SAM) SPADE, JO BELT'S FATHER, WHO ALSO SERVED IN THE ARMY AIR CORPS DURING WWII.

This is a story about five friends who served in five different branches of the United States Armed Forces and how they saved our nation from a dastardly and down-right doomed disaster!

Chesty was a bulldog, not just ANY bulldog. Chesty was the Marine Corps bulldog mascot. He fought many battles. Chesty was a faithful dog and a proud Marine!

Then one day old Chesty the bulldog retired. He had served his country well and deserved some definite down-time. He wanted to relax. So Chesty moved into the White House and became the official White House pet.

He spent many a moment recalling his heroic happenings in history.

One day when Chesty the bulldog napped, he was awakened by strange sounds. There was banging and clanging and chiseling! He put his ear to the floor and, sure enough, the sounds were coming from the White House basement!

Chesty ran to the top of the White House basement stairs. And what did he see? Rats! He almost barked out loud, "Oh my goodness, there are rats in the White House!" Those pesky rats were picking away at the precious golden bricks that are the foundation of our country! Liberty, Courage, Honor, Integrity, Hope!

The rats were going to replace the golden bricks with their own bricks. This would surely crumble the foundation of our nation!

Chesty ran to the White House back porch and watched as the rats carried away the golden bricks. Something had to be done—and NOW! He had to find and meet with his four military mascot friends fast!

Now, Joe the falcon wasn't just ANY falcon...Joe the falcon was the Air Force falcon mascot. He had flown many a mission in the skies and his legacy was long and proud. Joe was a fearless falcon.

Joe the falcon had retired and was spending his days relaxing in a tall tree on the grounds of a United States Air Force base. He was old and his wings were tired. He loved to day-dream about his daring deeds done while on active duty. Joe had been an Ace pilot...and proud of it!

"Oh Joe!" cried Chesty. "The nation needs your help! Come quickly! There are rats in the White House basement! And they plan to destroy our nation's foundation!"

Well, there was no stopping Joe the falcon from joining Chesty the bulldog. Joe the falcon loved his country – and hated rats! "Why sure I'll help!" answered Joe the falcon. "This is a job for all five branches of the military. I'll go get Bill the goat, Cutter the bear and Mr. Jackson the mule! I'll meet you back at the White House to plan our strategy!"

And away he flew!

Now Bill the goat, wasn't just ANY goat...Bill the goat was the Navy goat mascot. He had sailed the seas all over the world protecting our country, as well as other countries. Bill was a gutsy goat!

Bill the goat had retired and was spending his days grazing in the grass on a United States Naval base. Bill remembered fondly his selfless service while sailing the seas.

"Oh Bill!" cried Joe the falcon. "The nation needs your help! Come quickly! There are rats in the White House basement! And they plan to destroy our nation's foundation!"

Well, there was no stopping Bill the goat from joining Chesty the bulldog and Joe the falcon. Bill the goat loved his country – and hated rats! "Why sure I'll help!" answered Bill. "Count me IN!"

"Head for the White House!" said Joe the falcon. "We'll plan our strategy!"

And away he flew!

Now Cutter the bear wasn't just ANY bear...Cutter the bear was the Coast Guard bear mascot. He had defended our nation's shores and waterways for many years. Cutter was a very brave bear.

Cutter the bear had retired and was spending his days doing what he loved most – fishing. He lived on a Coast Guard boat and fished all day long. Cutter marveled at his many memories of mighty missions over the years.

"Oh Cutter!" cried Joe the falcon. "The nation needs your help! Come quickly! There are rats in the White House basement! And they plan to destroy our nation's foundation!"

Well, there was no stopping Cutter the bear from joining Chesty the bulldog, Joe the falcon and Bill the goat. Cutter loved his country – and hated rats!

"Why sure I'll help!" answered Cutter the bear. "Count me IN!"

"Head for the White House!" cried Joe the falcon. "We'll plan our strategy!"

And away he flew!

Now Mr. Jackson the mule wasn't just ANY mule. Mr. Jackson the mule was the Army mule mascot. He had travelled the world defending freedom and helping other countries, as well as his own. Mr. Jackson was a mighty mule!

Mr. Jackson the mule had retired and was living on a United States Army base. He grazed in the pasture and occasionally gave rides to the children of Army soldiers. The children loved him and he loved them. Mr. Jackson regularly reminisced regarding his daring deeds of duty.

"Oh Mr. Jackson!" cried Joe the falcon. "The nation needs your help! Come quickly! There are rats in the White House basement! And they plan to destroy our nation's foundation!"

Well, there was no stopping Mr. Jackson the mule from joining Chesty the bulldog, Joe the falcon, Bill the goat and Cutter the bear. Mr. Jackson loved his country – and hated rats!

"Why sure I'll help!" answered Mr. Jackson the mule. "Count me IN!"

"Head for the White House!" cried Joe the falcon. "We'll plan our strategy!"

And away he flew!

On his way to the White House, Joe the falcon spotted the rats down below. "Yikes!" Joe cried. "They're going to throw the golden bricks into the Potomac River! I must tell Chesty about this!"

The mascots listened carefully as Chesty the bulldog explained the situation. This was serious business! Each mascot knew they had a job to do to rescue the golden bricks.

"I will send Air Force jets!" cried Joe the falcon.
"And I will send Navy Seals!" cried Bill the goat.
"And I will send Army tanks!" cried Mr. Jackson the mule.
"And I will send Coast Guard ships!" cried Cutter the bear.

"And I will send helicopters filled with Marines!" cried Chesty the bulldog. "Together we will capture those rotten rats and return the golden bricks to the White House basement! We have to have the foundation of our country secure! Those bricks are very important. They support our country's values that we were given in the Declaration of Independence. How dare those rotten rats try to destroy what the forefathers of our country built! There's no job too big for the five branches of the United States military!"

Oh those rats! Their time had come! All they could do was jump and run! Those rotten rats were really scared. They tossed the bricks into the air! Why all the rage? Just turn the page!

Oh what a sight to be seen! The Army tanks rolled over the hill! The Air Force jets soared through the skies! The Navy Seals rose out of the Potomac! The Coast Guard ships sailed straight towards the rats! The Marine helicopters hovered overhead!

What a mighty force to be reckoned with: all five branches of the United States military coming together!! What team work!

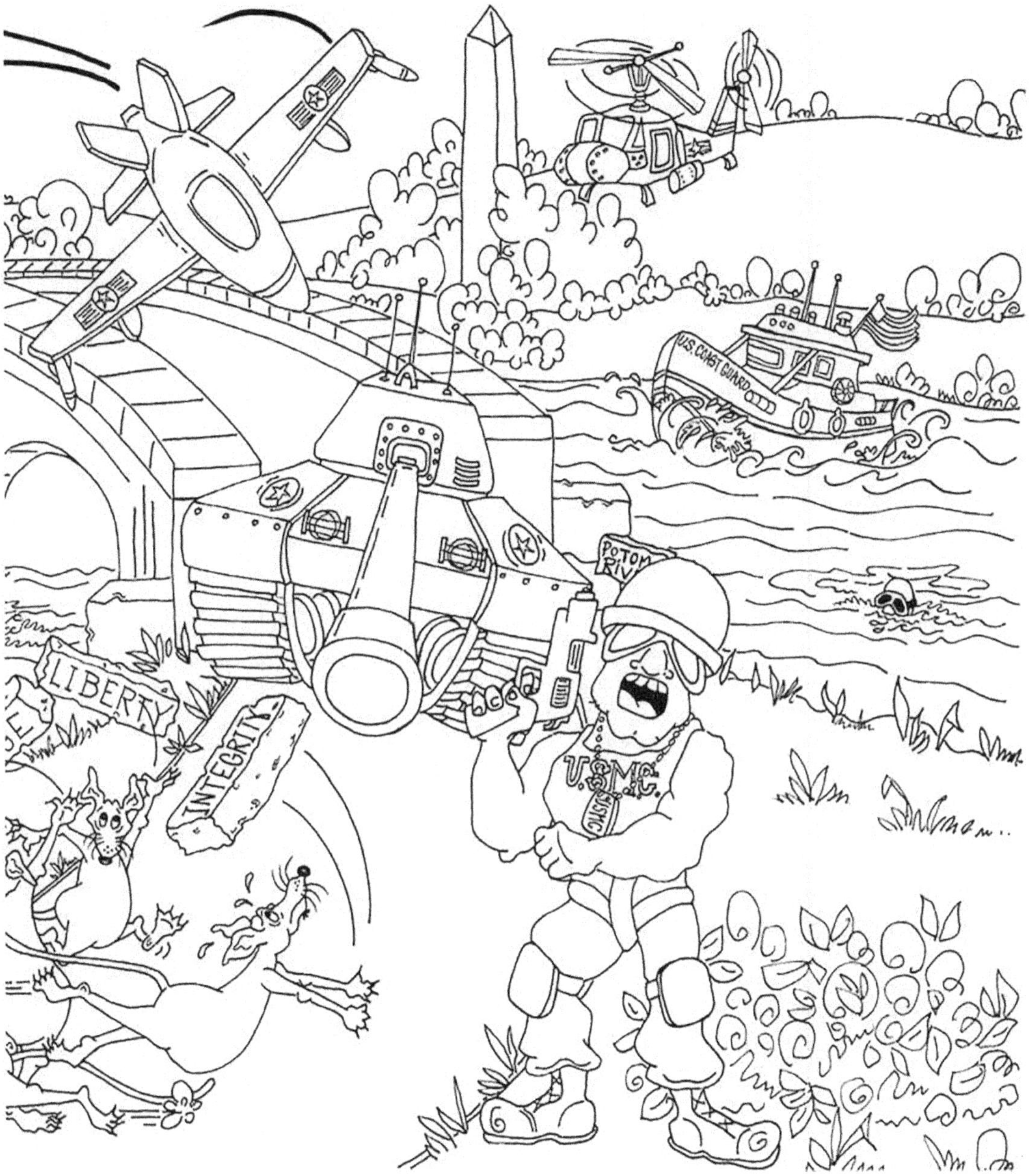

U.S. COAST GUARD
POTOM
RIV
LIBERTY
INTEGRITY
U.S.M.C.

Quickly Joe the falcon, Mr. Jackson the mule, Bill the goat and Cutter the bear grabbed those golden bricks and ran lickety-split to the White House. The 5 golden bricks sparkled as they once again supported the foundation of our nation.

Meanwhile, Chesty the bulldog had big plans for the raggedy, rotten rodents!

To the Slammer, Up the River, Behind Bars, to the Can!
You can bet this was not in the rats' master plan!
To the Big House, the Pokey, the Cooler, the Clink!
Their destruction ends NOW, those rotten rats stink!

The mission was a success. Those rats had failed! Locked away in jail, they will never again scheme against our great nation and chip away our country's foundation!

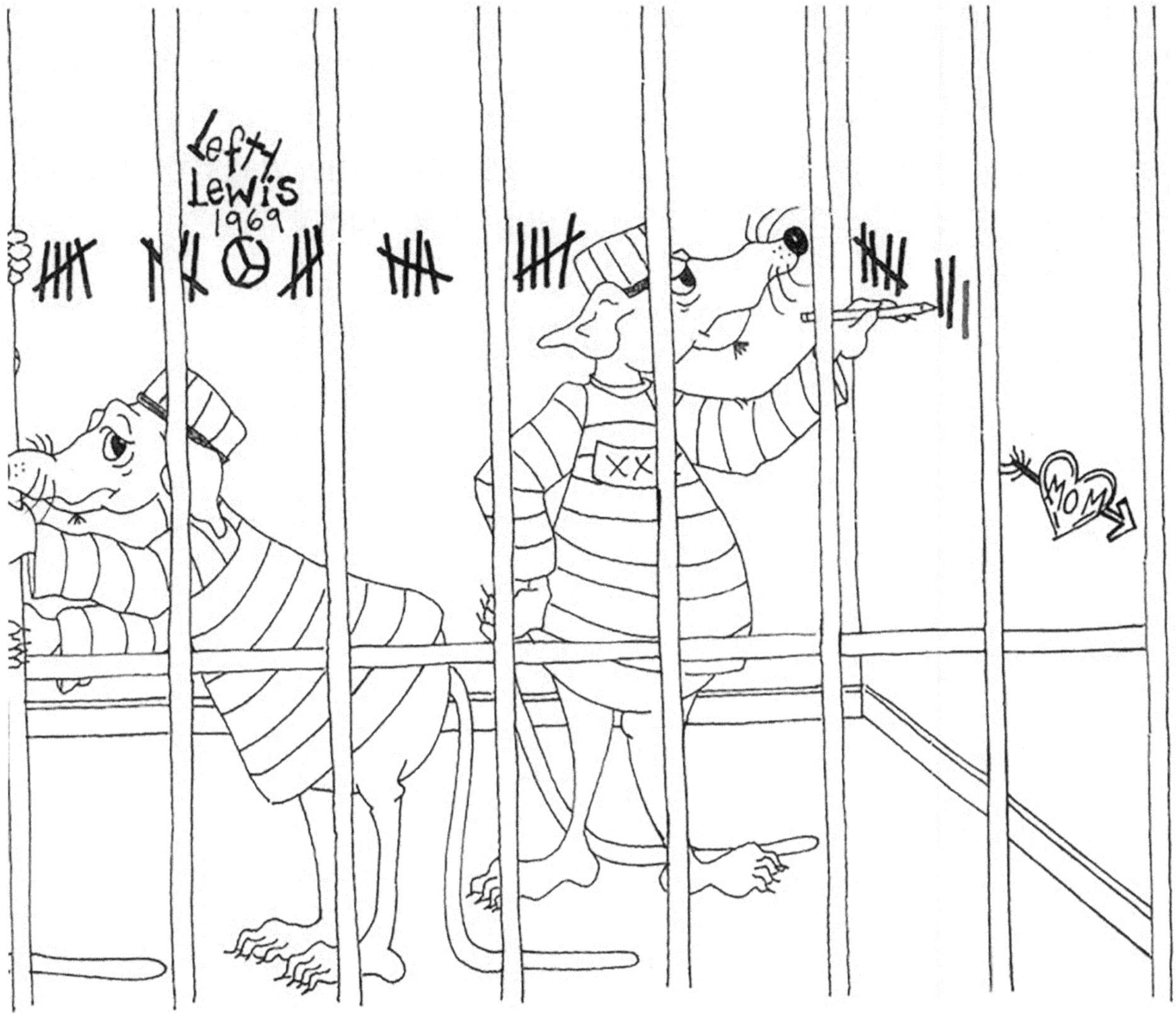
Lefty
Lewis
1969
XX
MOM

The five furry and faithful friends stood at attention on the steps of the United States Capitol building as they proudly accepted their Congressional Medals of Honor. Together, they had returned the golden bricks: Honor, Hope, Freedom, Integrity and Courage back into the walls of the White House foundation. The nation stood strong once again!

Then back to retirement each one went.

Those five Mascot Heroes – forever ready to defend our nation with their bravery and love for their country.

But then, you just never know when our nation will, once again, need their help!

THE END

THE PLEDGE OF ALLEGIANCE

I PLEDGE ALLEGIANCE TO THE FLAG OF
THE UNITED STATES OF AMERICA,
AND TO THE REPUBLIC FOR WHICH IT
STANDS, ONE NATION, UNDER GOD
INDIVISIBLE, WITH LIBERTY AND JUSTICE FOR ALL

"THE STAR SPANGLED BANNER"

The National Anthem consists of four verses. On almost every occasion only the first verse is sung.

Oh, say can you see by the dawn's early light. What so proudly we hailed at the twilight's last gleaming.Whose broad stripes and bright stars thru the perilous fight, O'er the ramparts we watched were so gallantly streaming. And the rockets' red glare, the bombs bursting in air, gave proof through the night that our flag was still there. Oh, say does that star-spangled banner yet waveO'er the land of the free and the home of the brave.

From the Halls of Montezuma to the Shores of Tripoli, We fight our country's battles on the land as on the sea. First to fight for right and freedom, And to keep our honor clean, we are proud to claim the title of United States Marine.

The "Marines' Hymn"

AIR FORCE SONG

Off we go into the wild blue yonder, Climbing high into the sun; here they come zooming to meet our thunder, at em boys, give'er the gun! Down we dive, spouting our flame from under, off with one hell of a roar! We live in fame or go down in flame.

Nothing'll stop the U.S. Air Force!

"The Navy Song"

Anchors Aweigh, my boys Anchors Aweigh. Farewell to college joys.
We sail at break of day, day, day, day. Through our last night ashore.
Drink to the foam Until we meet once more. Here's
wishing you a happy voyage home!

The Coast Guard Song "Semper Paratus"

From Aztec Shore to Arctic Zone, To Europe and Far East, The Flag is carried by our shipsin times of war and peace; and never have we struck it yet. In spite of foemen's might, who cheered our crews and cheered again for showing how to fight.
We're always ready for the call, we place our trust in Thee. Through surf and storm and howling gale, high shall our purpose be. "Semper Paratus" is our guide, our fame, our glory too. To fight to save or fight and die, Aye! Coast Guard we are for you!

The Army Song
"The Army Goes Rolling Along"

March along, sing our song, with the Army of the free. Count the brave, count the true, who have fought to victory. We're the Army and proud of our name. We're the Army and proudly proclaim.
First to fight for the right, and to build the Nation's might, and the Army Goes rolling along. Proud of all we have done, fighting till the battle's won, and the Army Goes Rolling Along.
Then it's Hi! Hi! Hey! The Army's on its way.
Count off the cadence loud and strong!
For where e'er we go, you will always know,
that the Army Goes Rolling Along.

THE MEDAL OF HONOR

ABOUT THE AUTHOR

Diann Wall Wilson is a published author and owner of 5 military mascot copyrights. She lives in Scottsdale, Arizona with her husband Bill. They have one daughter. Ann and one Granddaughter, Maddie.

ABOUT THE ILLUSTRATOR

Jo Belt is an Illustrator and muralist. Jo lives in Scottsdale, Arizona with her husband Robert. They have one daughter, Paige.

Milton Keynes UK
Ingram Content Group UK Ltd.
UKHW011253260824
447289UK00014B/51